Other Books by
R.L. STINE

SERIES:

- Goosebumps
- Fear Street
- Rotten School
- Mostly Ghostly

INDIVIDUAL TITLES:

- *It's the First Day of School…Forever!*
- *The Haunting Hour*
- *The Nightmare Hour*
- *Zombie Town*
- *The Adventures of Shrinkman*
- *The Creatures from Beyond Beyond*
- *Three Faces of Me*
- *My Alien Parents*

THE 13TH WARNING

two lions

Text copyright © 2000 Parachute Press
Cover illustration by Tim Jacobus

A Parachute Press Book

Published by Amazon Publishing
P.O. Box 400818
Las Vegas, NV 89140

ISBN-13: 9781612183305
ISBN-10: 1612183301

R.L. STINE

THE 13TH WARNING

two lions

INTRODUCTION

· **R.L. STINE** ·

Before I talk about how I got the idea for this book, let me ask you a question:

Are you superstitious?

Do you walk *around* ladders, never under them? Do you knock wood? Toss salt over your shoulder? Say "bless you" when someone sneezes? Hold your breath when you pass a cemetery? Stay home on Friday the thirteenth?

Those are all superstitions. They are supposed to keep the bad luck spirits away.

When my brother Bill and I were kids, we would walk home after school. Some afternoons, as we made our way along the sidewalks, we would chant this rhyme:

Step on a crack. Break your mother's back.

I don't know if we really believed it or not. But we both hopped and jumped and twisted and slid—and did our very best not to step on a crack. Of course one of us *always* slipped up and stepped on a sidewalk crack. Somehow our mother survived with her back in pretty good shape.

We were very superstitious kids. Whenever we saw a black cat, we ran away screaming. And when my dad dropped a mirror and it shattered into a million pieces, Bill and I were convinced our family would have seven years of bad luck.

Now, as an adult, I don't have any superstitions at all. Well…maybe a few.

I guess my biggest superstition is about New York City. I have lived in New York City for many years, and I love it. I think it's the most interesting and exciting city in the world.

But I have *never* written a book for kids that takes place in New York.

Why? I can't really explain it. I just have a feeling it's unlucky. Maybe the book would be a flop. Maybe something bad would happen to me while I was writing it. I know it's a crazy superstition. But I don't want to test it. I won't write a New York City book—ever.

I think about good luck and bad luck a lot. Some people have good luck charms—things they wear or carry with them to bring them luck. This made me think: Is there such a thing as a *bad* luck charm?

I wrote a Goosebumps book called *It Came from Beneath the Sink*. It was about a family that moved to a new house. While they were exploring, they found a dried-up sponge under the kitchen sink. They didn't know it, but the sponge was an evil bad luck charm.

Horrible things started to happen. Accidents. Injuries. Terrible, painful falls. If the family had taken a close look at the sponge, they would have seen it had eyes and teeth! Their big problem: How do you get rid of a bad luck charm? Are you stuck with it forever?

Of course the most popular superstition has to do with the number 13. Lots of people agree the number is very unlucky. And for many, Friday the thirteenth is the most frightening, unluckiest day on the calendar. This superstition even has a name. It's called *triskaidekaphobia*.

How unlucky would it be to live or work on the thirteenth floor of a building? Most people don't want to find out. That's why most skyscrapers and apartment buildings in the United States don't have a thirteenth floor. The elevators go right from 12 to 14.

When I visited China to meet my Goosebumps readers there, I was surprised when the kids I met told me their unlucky number is 4. The number 4 is pronounced very much like the word for *death*, so that makes it a scary number. Buildings in China don't have a fourth floor!

Where did the superstition about the number 13 come from? How did it start? I haven't been able to find a good reason. People have all kinds of crazy ideas about it.

Some say it started because there are thirteen moons during the year, and people are afraid of the full moon. The craziest idea I read was that number 13 scares people because it's the first number you can't count using your ten fingers and two feet. Does that make any sense? I don't think so.

But it's fun to have a number that frightens everyone. My first book about this superstition was *Locker 13*, in my Nightmare Room book series. A new kid in school gets the last remaining locker. Sure enough, it's locker number 13. And sure enough, his luck instantly changes, from good to bad to *horrible!*

What he doesn't realize is there's an evil creature *living inside the locker,* waiting to pull him into a terrifying world. If you have a school locker with the number 13 on the door, my advice to you is keep it locked during the day—and *don't ever open it in the dark!*

The 13ᵗʰ Warning is a book with so many thirteens in it, it *has* to be scary! The idea came to me at a friend's house. He brought out his new black cat. The cat was named—guess what?—Lucky.

Lucky stared at me with his glowing green eyes, and I stared back. And suddenly I had the idea for this book. What if there is a kid who is always so lucky his friends call him Lucky? But what if he's in danger of losing all his luck?

The boy is the thirteenth child of two thirteenth children. And if he doesn't watch out for the number 13, his thirteenth birthday may be his last!

Enjoy the book. I guarantee you'll find at least thirteen scares in it!

R L Stine

CHAPTER 1

Do you want to hear a terrifying story about bad luck?

Well, you've come to the wrong place.

You won't hear it from me—because I'm one of the luckiest people I know.

In fact, no one calls me by my real name—Joe. Everyone calls me Lucky.

I'm the thirteenth child of two thirteenth children! That's right. I have twelve older brothers and sisters. And my mom and dad each have twelve older brothers and sisters.

That's triple thirteen. You can't get any luckier than that—can you?

To top it off, I was born on the thirteenth of the month.

How lucky am I? Well…my mom never calls me to dinner in the middle of my favorite TV show. Coin tosses almost always go my way. The teacher never asks to see my homework when I don't have it. I'm always the winner on phone-in radio station contests.

You know how some people feel about the number thirteen. They think it's really *un*lucky. So they call me Lucky as a joke.

I don't mind. Actually, I think it's kind of cool.

So do my parents. They're really into the whole thirteen thing. Guess what our address is? That's right! 13 Horseshoe Lane.

"You should stop bragging about all your good luck," my sister Lindy said. "Your thirteenth birthday is tomorrow. What if your luck suddenly changes?"

"Ha ha," I replied. "Ha ha."

Famous last words.

CHAPTER 2

Lindy isn't as lucky as me. That's because she's kid number twelve.

What kind of number is twelve? Bor-ing!

"Mom said we should talk about your cake," Lindy said.

"What about my cake?" I glanced up from my math book.

I was trying to study math. Even a kid as lucky as me has to study sometimes.

Lindy sighed. "Mom has to call the restaurant. To tell them if you want anything special on your cake tomorrow."

I glanced up from my math book. "It's going to be awesome, isn't it? Having my party at the Lucky Duck."

The Lucky Duck Diner is the best. Not just because of the name. They have really cool outdoor tables set up on a brick patio. Twinkling lights are strung up in the branches of the trees all around. And there's a pond with live ducks in it that swim past your table.

And they have the best pizza in the world. You can't have a birthday dinner without pizza—right?

I leaned back in my chair, thinking about that pizza. My elbow hit my math book and knocked it off my desk. The book fell with a *thump*—onto my dog Barker's paw.

Barker was sleeping, as usual. She's getting old, so she sleeps a lot. She awoke with a start when the book hit her.

"Oops! Sorry, Barker," I apologized. I leaned over and gave her a pat.

Most dogs would bark if they got banged by a falling book. Not Barker. That's the weird thing about her. She *never* barks.

You guessed it—that's why my parents named her Barker. Funny, huh?

She's a cool dog. She's always been more mine than anyone else's. You might say we grew up together.

I glanced at the old wooden clock on my dresser. And gasped. "Oh, no!" I leaped up. This time my English book went flying. Barker moved away just in time.

"What's wrong?" Lindy asked.

I grabbed my gym bag. "It's five o'clock. Swim practice started at four-thirty. Coach Macker will be furious!"

Lindy grabbed me as I rushed past. She pointed to her watch. "It's only four. You've got plenty of time. Your stupid clock is messed up. As usual."

I glanced at my wristwatch. Four o'clock. She was right.

I sighed. "I'd better reset it." I picked up the clock. My uncle Ted gave it to me. It's a great old clock. But it always runs too slow or too fast.

It's supposed to chime. But the chimes hardly ever go off at the right time. Sometimes they don't go off at all. And once it chimed eleven o'clock twice in a row. At three in the morning!

I wound the clock and set it on my desk.

The doorbell rang. Lindy and I hurried downstairs. Barker plodded after us.

"It's probably the post office delivering more birthday presents!" I said.

"Like you need more!" Lindy groaned.

I grinned. The hall closet was packed with gifts for me. Having twenty-four aunts and uncles is awesome at birthday time!

But I was wrong. It wasn't a gift being delivered.

It was the beginning of a horror story.

CHAPTER 3

A man and woman stood on the doorstep.

The man was old. I mean ancient. His skin was withered and wrinkled, like a dry prune. And deathly pale against his black clothes.

His dark, hollow eyes were sunk so deep they looked like empty black holes in his face. He smiled, and I saw his teeth—yellowed and broken.

The woman was younger. But just as creepy. Her skin was paler than a dead fish. She had stringy orange hair and watery blue eyes that bulged out of her head. She was dressed all in black, too.

To make things even stranger, the woman had a huge black cat perched on her shoulder.

Barker poked her head out the door. She spotted the cat and growled. She may be old, but she still loves to chase cats.

The cat's yellow eyes narrowed. But it didn't move.

I grabbed Barker's collar. "Can I help you?" I asked.

The strangers stared hard at me. As if studying me.

"Are you Joseph?" the man finally asked. His voice was thin and hoarse. "The thirteenth child?"

"Joseph?" No one calls me Joseph. Even my teachers call me Lucky. "Uh, yeah, that's me," I said.

"What do you want?" Lindy demanded from behind me.

"We're from the Superstition Society," the woman announced. "We came to warn you."

"Warn me? What are you talking about?" I asked.

"You have tempted the spirits of evil!" The old man wheezed. He took a step closer. "You have too many thirteens. Too many!"

I backed away. The guy was definitely creepy.

"I happen to like thirteens," I declared. "Thirteen is my lucky number. What's wrong with that?"

The woman frowned. "You don't understand," she said softly. "You're in danger, Joseph. Tomorrow is your thirteenth birthday, right?"

"Right," I replied.

"Well, we have to warn you. If you collect a total of thirteen thirteens before midnight tomorrow, the evil spirits will be unleashed. They'll come for you!"

I felt a chill. Who were these weirdos? How did they know it was my birthday tomorrow?

"Beware!" the old man whispered. "The darkness brings evil. The evil will come for you!"

The black cat started hissing. It dug its claws into the woman's shoulder. The hairs along its spine bristled.

"The cat senses that you are in danger. Danger!" the old woman said.

The old man fixed his black eyes on mine. "Beware, Joseph. Beware of the thirteens. Your luck—it is running out."

They turned and hobbled away.

"Wait—!" I cried. "Hey, wait! I don't understand!"

But only the black cat turned back. And it opened its mouth in one last, frightening hiss.

CHAPTER 4

Trembling, I slammed the front door shut.

"They're crazy," Lindy snorted. "I mean, evil spirits? Come on! No wonder everyone makes fun of the Superstition Society. And can you believe the way they were dressed?"

I bit my lip. "You think I should ignore them?" I asked.

"No," Lindy said. "I think their visit makes a great story. You should save it to tell at your party tomorrow night."

My party. "Hey, I just got a great idea!" I cried. "Let's ask the Lucky Duck to make my cake in the shape of the number thirteen. Wouldn't that be cool?"

"Totally!" Lindy agreed. "Mom isn't home. I'll call them right now!"

I led the way into the living room. I hurried toward the phone on the coffee table.

My sneaker caught on the edge of the rug. I tripped and fell. My shoulder crashed against the low table.

And sent my mom's brand-new glass vase flying!

No problem. I was lucky, right?

I reached out to catch the vase.

CRASH!

The vase slipped through my fingers. It shattered into pieces on the hardwood floor.

"Oh, no." Lindy groaned. "You broke Mom's new vase!"

I couldn't believe it. I stared at the broken glass in shock.

"You had it right in your hands. You should have caught that!" Lindy cried.

"No kidding," I muttered.

"Hi, gang! I'm home!" a cheerful voice called.

"Uh-oh," Lindy whispered. "Mom!"

I gulped. This was bad. Mom hates when things get broken. You'd think with thirteen kids she'd be used to it. No way.

"Kids?" Mom called. "Anybody here?"

She stuck her head into the living room. And gasped when she saw the mess.

"Hi, Mom," I said weakly. "I…uh…had a little accident."

"That vase was brand new!" Mom said, shaking her head. "It was a gift from my cousin Marci."

That made me feel even worse. Cousin Marci lives in Canada. Mom never gets to see her.

"Sorry," I muttered. "I tripped on the rug."

Mom stared at me. I waited for her to freak out. But she laughed instead. "Actually, I thought it was the ugliest vase I ever saw!"

Whew! A close one.

"Just clean up this mess, and we'll pretend it never happened," Mom said. She turned and headed to the kitchen.

"You lucked out this time," Lindy whispered. "As usual!"

There was just one problem. By the time I finished cleaning up, I was late leaving for swim practice.

I biked over to the pool as fast as I could. It usually takes a while for everyone to get changed and warmed up. I figured, with luck, I'd catch up before Coach started the practice.

But when I reached the pool, practice was under way. And Coach Macker looked angry. "You're late, Lucky. Get changed. You owe me an extra twenty laps."

"Busted!" whispered my teammate, Alex. "Bad luck, man."

I frowned at him. For a second I heard that weird old man's voice again: *Your luck is running out…*

I shook my head. No way did I believe that crazy warning.

The rest of practice went great. I won every heat I swam in. If it was a meet, I would have won a whole load of trophies.

After practice I changed back into my clothes. I headed out of the locker room with the rest of the team. Coach was waiting for us outside.

"Hold up, guys," he called. "Our new team jerseys just arrived!" He waved toward a big cardboard box. It sat at the edge of the pool, near the deep end.

"Finally," Alex muttered to me. "Coach has been talking about those jerseys for weeks."

We all gathered around. Coach started passing out the green and white jerseys. Finally he called my name. "Lucky, I saved the last jersey especially for you."

He pulled out a shirt and tossed it to me.

I unfolded it. On the back was a giant number thirteen. Way cool!

"Thanks, Coach," I said. "This will really bring me luck."

I started to pull it over my head. It caught in my hair.

I gave it a hard tug. My sneakers slipped on the wet tile floor.

I fell forward.

"Lucky!" Alex yelled. *"Look out!"*

CHAPTER 5

"Whoa!"

I teetered on the pool edge for a second. My arms whirled in the air like windmills.

Then I toppled into the pool, sending up a tall wave of water.

Down…down to the bottom.

I could feel my sneakers fill with water. My shorts swelled up with air and floated around me. I was so surprised, I gulped a large mouthful of water and started to choke.

Can't breathe…Can't breathe…

Choking, sputtering, I kicked my way up to the surface.

The others were laughing as I dragged myself out of the pool. I sucked in breath after breath of air. My heart was pounding like crazy.

"You need to work on that dive!" Coach Macker joked.

Everyone laughed even more.

I did my best to wring out my sopping clothes. I checked my watch. It was still ticking. That was lucky.

But I wasn't feeling real lucky at the moment. Falling into the pool in my clothes in front of the whole swim team isn't exactly lucky.

I pedaled home as fast as I could. I wanted to get into dry clothes. But Lindy was just leaving for a bike ride. I needed to talk to her, so I tagged along.

Barker came, too. She loves to follow when we go bike riding. But she has trouble keeping up lately.

"I want to ask you something," I said. "I know it's kind of dumb…"

"What's the problem now?" Lindy asked as we pedaled slowly up the road.

I glanced behind us. Barker was panting. She jogged along for a few more steps, then turned and trotted toward home.

"That old couple," I said. "Do you think they could be telling the truth? That my luck is running out?"

Lindy tilted her head at me. "Not really. In fact I think it's kind of dumb," she said. "What happened at swim practice? You didn't win any races?"

"No. I won them all," I said.

She tossed back her head and laughed. "You won them all, and you think your luck is running out?"

I could feel my face turning hot. I knew I was blushing. "You're right," I said. "I won't think about it again."

I let out a cry as my bike shuddered hard.

A hole in the road?

I never even saw it!

The front wheel jerked sharply to the left. The bike pitched forward.

I opened my mouth in a startled scream as I went flying over the handlebars.

CHAPTER 6

I landed hard on my side. And let out a groan as pain shot through my body.

My elbow throbbed. My arm was scraped raw. My T-shirt was streaked with dirt and tar.

Lindy leaped off her bike and ran over to me. "Are you okay?"

I sat up slowly, my head spinning. "I think so," I muttered. I glanced at my bike. The front tire had ripped open on the edge of that stupid pothole. The wheel was totally bent. The chain had fallen off.

"Maybe someone got you a new bike for your birthday," Lindy murmured.

I sighed. "I don't think so."

I stood up shakily and limped over to my bike. My left ankle ached. Blood trickled from the cut on my arm.

Lindy and I turned our bikes toward home. We walked in silence.

"I know what you're thinking," Lindy said. "But I still think the warning from those weird people is a bunch of baloney." She paused. "But maybe we should count your thirteens. You know. Just in case. How many do you actually have?"

I was already counting in my head. "I'm the thirteenth kid of two thirteenth kids," I recited. "That's three right there."

"And you're turning thirteen on the thirteenth," Lindy added. "That's two more. Five thirteens."

I felt my heart beat a little faster. "And there's my new swim team number," I told her. "That's six."

"Six. That's not so many." Lindy smiled. "Hey, your birthday is tomorrow, right? *No way* you can get seven more thirteens in just one day."

"I guess not," I agreed. "That would be an awful lot. Even for me!"

I felt a lot better.

We turned the corner onto our block. I spotted the mailbox at the end of our driveway.

I stopped short.

"Oh, no!" I groaned.

CHAPTER 7

I read our address on the mailbox: 13 Horseshoe Lane.

"Seven," I said. "Seven thirteens!" My stomach started to churn.

Lindy put a hand on my shoulder. "Take it easy, Lucky," she said. "You still have six to go. *If* you believe that goofy warning."

"Right," I muttered. I wasn't sure what to believe.

Lindy and I left our bikes by the garage and made our way into the kitchen. The rest of my family was getting ready for dinner.

Mom gasped when she saw me. "Lucky! What happened to you?"

My seventeen-year-old twin brothers glanced up from setting the table. Johnny stared. "Whoa! Look what the cat shouldn't have dragged in!"

"I like your new look!" Jimmy teased.

I ignored them. "I fell off my bike," I told Mom. "I'm going upstairs to change."

When I came back, the others were already eating.

"Sit down, Lucky," Dad urged. "We're having your favorite."

"Bacon burgers! Cool!" I exclaimed. At least something was going my way.

The burgers smelled great. I grabbed a thick one. I broke off a piece of bacon to slip to Barker. It's her favorite treat.

I glanced around.

She wasn't in the dining room.

That was weird. Barker hangs around the table at every mealtime. She's always begging for scraps. Especially when there's bacon involved.

"Where's Barker?" I asked.

Mom shot me a stern glance. "Don't start feeding that dog your dinner, Lucky," she warned. "She's fat enough as it is."

I dropped the bacon back on my plate. But I kept glancing around. "No, really," I insisted. "Where is she?"

My sister Andrea shrugged. "Maybe she's stuck in a closet. That dumb dog is always getting trapped. She should learn to bark. Then we wouldn't have this problem."

I leaped up from the table.

"Finish your dinner," Dad said. "Then we'll all help you find Barker."

I sat back down. But I wasn't happy about it.

I could barely eat. After dinner we searched the entire house, from attic to basement to garage.

No sign of Barker.

I started to get seriously worried. Did she ever come back from the bike ride?

As I was checking the hall closet for the third time, Lindy came up behind me. "Find her?"

"No. I think maybe something happened to her," I said in a trembling voice.

"I hope not," she murmured. "We've had Barker forever. I still remember when Mom and Dad got her. It was the same day they brought you home from the hospital. She was so cute!"

"Huh? Excuse me?" I stared at Lindy.

I felt a shiver run down my back. "Then Barker was already a puppy when I was born," I began. "That means she's a couple of months older than me."

Which meant she was thirteen years old.

That made eight. Eight thirteens.

The phone rang.

I grabbed it. Maybe one of the neighbors found Barker. "Hello?" I said eagerly.

But it was Coach Macker. "Lucky, glad I caught you. I forgot to get your Social Security number at practice. I need it for our new computer system."

I had no idea what my Social Security number was. And right now I was so worried about Barker, I couldn't care less.

"Hold on, Coach," I said. I handed the phone to Lindy. "Don't hang up. I'll be right back."

I found Dad in the garage. I told him what Coach Macker needed.

"No problem," Dad said. "Follow me."

I followed him inside. Dad grabbed a file out of the desk in the kitchen. He shuffled through a stack of papers inside.

"Here we go." Dad grabbed the kitchen phone. "Coach? Got it right here." He glanced down at the paper in his hand. "It's six eighty-one, thirteen, seventy-two…"

My heart stopped.

No!

Not *another* thirteen!

CHAPTER 8

I rushed back to the living room. "Lindy!" I called. "I've got another thirteen! It's in my Social Security number!"

Lindy's eyes widened. "That's nine," she breathed. Nine thirteens.

"This is starting to get scary," Lindy said softly. "You only have four thirteens left."

"Tell me something I don't know!" I groaned. "But that's not important. We—we have to find Barker!"

I borrowed my brother Johnny's bike. Lindy came with me. We rode all over the neighborhood, searching every place we could think of, calling our dog's name.

No luck.

At bedtime Barker was still missing. I tossed and turned in bed. I couldn't sleep. Not while Barker was missing.

*Tick…tick…tick…*My old clock seemed noisier than usual.

One…two…three…I counted in my head.

Then I realized what I was doing. Cut it out! I told myself. Worrying about thirteens is totally stupid!

Finally I started to drift off to sleep. My mind got fuzzy and started to go blank.

WRRRUOUFF!

The sound jolted me awake. It came from right outside my window.

WRRRUOUFF! WRRRUOUFF!

A dog bark?

I leaped out of bed and raced to the window. My heart was pounding. Not with fear—with hope.

WRRRUOUFF!

"Barker!" I cried.

She was right below my window. Barking her brains out. I was so happy, I started to do a crazy dance.

WRRRUOUFF! WRRRUOUFF!

"I'm coming, girl!" I shouted to her.

Her tail wagged at my voice. She kept barking.

WRRUOUFF.

I laughed. Maybe Barker had never barked before. But she was sure making up for it now!

"All right, all right! I'm coming," I repeated. I whirled and raced for the hall.

WRRRUOUFF!

"Eight barks," I murmured. I was so used to counting, I couldn't stop.

WRRRUOUFF!

I crashed into Lindy at the top of the stairs.

"Is that Barker?" she asked, rubbing her sleepy-looking eyes.

"It's her, all right!" I said.

"I can't believe she's barking," Lindy remarked. "It's really weird."

WRRRUOUFF!

I gulped. "Ten," I counted.

Lindy's eyes widened. She guessed why I was counting.

WRRRUOUFF!

"Uh-oh," Lindy murmured.

We took the stairs two at a time. My heart was pounding. I had to stop Barker. Before she barked two more times!

I tried to take the steps three at a time. But I slipped and skidded down the last step. I landed hard on my left ankle. The same ankle I hurt falling off my bike.

"Yeeowch!" I cried. I staggered toward the front door.

WRRRUOUFF!

That was twelve barks!

I grabbed for the dead bolt—and jammed my thumb on the door frame. Ow!

I grasped the lock and twisted. But the bolt still wouldn't turn. What was wrong with it? Why wouldn't it open?

"You're turning it the wrong way!" Lindy shouted.

Finally I heard the lock click. I flung the door open.

Barker was sitting on the front lawn. She opened her mouth.

I lunged forward.

"No, Barker!" I shouted. "Quiet, girl. Don't bark. Please, don't bark!"

CHAPTER 9

WRROUFFFF!

I froze in horror.

"Thirteen," I whispered. "That makes ten thirteens!"

"Wait!" Lindy commanded. She grabbed my arm. "Let Barker bark a few more times. Then it won't mean anything."

Hey! She was right!

I stared at Barker. Come on, girl, bark! I thought.

Barker stared back. She opened her mouth...

And sneezed.

She whined, then heaved herself to her feet. Pushing past us into the kitchen, she began lapping water from her bowl.

I gulped. "Uh-oh."

Lindy didn't say anything. She didn't look at me. But I knew what she was thinking.

Ten thirteens.

Only three left.

The homeroom bell rang as I slid into my seat. It was my birthday, but I couldn't think about that. I couldn't stop thinking about my ten thirteens.

What if the prediction by the Superstition Society *was* true? What if I got three more thirteens before midnight?

Math was my first class of the day.

Uh-oh! I realized. I never did finish my homework.

If we had a pop quiz today, I was in major trouble.

But this morning my luck held. No quiz. My teacher was out sick. We had a substitute named Mrs. Kline.

Someone told Mrs. Kline it was my birthday. "Really?" she chirped. "That's wonderful! Let's have a party!"

The other kids cheered. All right! No quiz—and no math class, either! Now, that was lucky!

"Wait quietly for a moment, people. I'm going to go make a phone call," Mrs. Kline told us. "My husband owns a bakery. I bet he'll send over something for our birthday celebration. What's your favorite treat, Lucky?"

"Glazed doughnuts," I replied.

"Coming right up!" the teacher said.

I sat back in my seat and smiled. This was so great! It was really starting to feel like my birthday.

Maybe I've been worrying over nothing, I thought. Maybe my luck hasn't changed after all!

Ten minutes later a delivery man arrived with a huge box from the bakery. There were cookies and cupcakes for the class. And a special gift-wrapped box for me.

"There you go, Lucky," Mrs. Kline said. "A special present for a special birthday. A baker's dozen doughnuts."

I eagerly tore open the box. It was filled to the top with delicious-looking glazed doughnuts. "Awesome!" I cried. "Thanks."

I picked one up and bit into it. It was still warm from the oven. Mmmmmm. The best doughnut I ever tasted!

I finished that doughnut and two more.

Nine doughnuts left, I thought.

Wait a minute. I checked the box.

There were *ten* left!

I counted again. Ten doughnuts left. But that meant...

"Didn't you say there were a dozen doughnuts in here?" I asked the teacher.

She smiled at me. "That's right. A baker's dozen."

"Um, a baker's dozen?" I repeated. "You mean twelve?"

"Oh, no," she chirped. "A regular dozen means twelve. A baker's dozen means *thirteen*."

CHAPTER 10

A baker's dozen means thirteen.

The teacher's cheery voice echoed in my head.

Thirteen doughnuts.

That meant I was up to eleven.

Only two more to go.

For the rest of the class I sat slumped in my chair. I hardly noticed what happened.

When the bell rang, I headed to my locker to get books for my English class. At least I would have time to think there. Miss Evans, my English teacher, was great. She never even checked our homework. That was a good thing. I was at least six chapters behind in our reading.

I spun the combination lock and swung open the locker. My English book was crammed near the bottom of a huge pile of stuff. I pulled it out.

The pile shuddered. And shifted…

Avalanche!

Books, papers, and my gym shoes came crashing down.

"Whoa!" I leaned back quickly and tossed up my arms. "Ow!" I yelped as my science book bounced off my head.

I leaped aside just in time to avoid my history book. Whew! It weighed about thirty pounds.

The book landed behind me and bounced to the middle of the hall.

Just in time to trip Mr. Landers, my science teacher. He cried out in surprise and stumbled forward.

He was carrying something in his arms. Something big. And heavy. And made of glass.

It was our class project. A huge ant farm.

As he hit the floor, it flew out of his hands. And smashed against the wall of lockers.

I heard the crack of glass. And then sand, dirt, broken glass, and ants scattered everywhere.

"Ooooh!" Mr. Landers groaned. He sat up and rubbed his knee. Then he spotted me. "Lucky! Is that your book?"

I nodded. "It…uh…fell out of my locker," I said. "It was an accident. Sorry about that, Mr. Landers."

The teacher glared at me for a second. "It's your birthday today, isn't it?"

I nodded again.

"Then here's my gift to you," he snapped. "I'm *not* going to give you a hard time." He climbed to his feet with another groan. "I'm not even going to make you help clean up this mess."

"Thanks, Mr. Landers!" I exclaimed. "I guess I'd better get to class."

"Not so fast." Mr. Landers led me to my open locker. "First we're going to make sure this doesn't happen again. I'm going to stand here and watch while you straighten up that disaster area you call a locker."

I knew I'd be late for English. But I knew better than to argue with Mr. Landers. I got to work right away.

By the time I made it to English class, I was ten minutes late.

"Lucky, glad you could make it," Miss Evans said as I entered. "Sit down. We're taking a test."

A test? "B-but we aren't supposed to have a test today!" I stammered.

"I know," she replied. "But some of you have been slacking off on your reading. So we're having a pop quiz. Just to make sure everyone read this week's assignment."

I slumped down in my seat. I hadn't read a word of the assignment. I'd flunk, for sure.

I took my best guess at the answers. Usually, my guesses turned out to be right.

But was my luck holding out?

I kept thinking about my eleven thirteens.

What would happen to me if I got two more?

"The evil will come for you," the old man had said.

What evil? What would it do?

After twenty minutes Miss Evans collected our test papers. She told us to read ahead in our books while she corrected them.

I opened my book. But I hardly saw the words on the page.

What would happen to me if that crazy warning came true?

I didn't want to find out.

I *had* to make it to midnight without collecting two more thirteens!

At the end of class Miss Evans handed back our tests. "I'm surprised at you, Lucky," she said, handing my paper to me.

I flipped my paper over.

My grade was scribbled in red ink at the top of the page.

I glanced at it. And choked.

CHAPTER 11

My score was a *thirteen*!

My throat felt so tight I couldn't breathe.

That made twelve thirteens.

Just one more to go.

How did I make it through the rest of the school day? I don't know.

I was too nervous and frightened to think straight. I could barely sit still.

At last the bell rang. I raced home. I found Lindy in the kitchen, pouring herself a glass of juice. I told her everything.

"Twelve thirteens." She tsk-tsked, shaking her head. "Wow."

"I wish my party wasn't tonight," I muttered. "Then I could lock myself in my room until midnight. Maybe then I'd be safe."

Mom and Dad walked into the room. "Safe from what?" Mom asked.

Dad grinned at me. "Hey, Birthday Boy. Are you looking forward to your party?"

"Well, uh, actually, I'm really not feeling too good," I said. "Maybe we should have my party next week instead."

Mom frowned. She put a hand on my forehead. "You don't have a fever," she said. "Is your throat sore?"

"Uh, no," I replied. "I mean, yes. I mean…"

My voice trailed off. Dad gave me a suspicious look. "What's this all about, Lucky?" he demanded.

I shot Lindy a helpless glance. She shrugged.

"Okay," I said with a sigh. "Here it is—the whole truth."

I told my parents all about my weird visitors. About all the bad luck I'd been having. And about the thirteens.

By the time I finished, Dad was staring hard at me. "You're kidding, right?" he said.

"I think I saw a movie like that," Mom said. "That's very creative, Lucky. Are you going to write it for English class?"

"You should tell it tonight at dinner," Dad said. "Everyone will get a kick out of it. It's a really creepy story."

They walked out of the room, talking about my story.

They didn't believe me.

"We're leaving in a few minutes. Better get ready," Dad called back to me.

I sighed. "I knew that they wouldn't believe me," I muttered.

"Not them," Lindy agreed. "They're the least superstitious people in the world."

"They'll never let me stay home." I shook my head. "That's it. I'm doomed!"

I counted everything I saw in the Lucky Duck Diner. Twenty-two guests. Six outdoor tables. Nine trees around the patio. Five big clouds in the sky. One sun. Seven waiters.

Everybody seemed to be having a great time. They ate. Laughed. Joked. Chatted.

I counted.

Eight slices in each pizza. Nine ice cubes in my soda. Fifteen blue bows on my presents.

I also counted the minutes. The time left until this party would be over. Until midnight.

Until I was safe.

Lindy was counting, too. "Only seven slices left over," she whispered as the waiter cleared away the pizza dishes. "So far, so good."

I nodded. I couldn't stop counting long enough to answer.

I got eleven computer games as gifts. Fourteen friends wore T-shirts. There were sixteen corn-rows in my friend Lucy's hair.

I glanced at my watch. It was almost ten o'clock. The moon was rising. The five clouds had become three clouds. Only two hours left until midnight...

Then I heard a noise at the other end of the restaurant. I turned to see what was happening. And let out a cry.

My dad was helping one of the waiters bring something out of the kitchen. Something on a big platter.

My birthday cake.

With thirteen candles burning on it!

CHAPTER 12

My heart stopped for a second. Then I felt it shoot up to my throat.

Lindy saw my expression. She shook her head.

"You're okay, Lucky. Count them," she whispered. "There are fourteen!"

Of course! One candle for each year. Plus one to grow on.

I counted them just to make sure. Yes! Fourteen candles.

I let out my breath in a long *whoosh*. I wiped my sweaty palms on my napkin.

I couldn't take another scare like that one!

Everyone sang "Happy Birthday." I blew out the candles.

I'll bet you know my wish—*no more thirteens!*

Finally it was time to go home. I glanced at my watch. Eleven o'clock. Just one hour till midnight. I slumped in relief.

My friends started leaving. As I said goodbye, I did my best to act normal. Some of my brothers and sisters left, too. Dad pulled out his wallet to pay the bill.

11:05.

The waiter brought Dad his receipt. My mom chatted with my oldest sister and her husband.

"Are we ever going to get out of here?" I moaned to Lindy.

"Hang in there, bro," she murmured.

11:10.

I couldn't stop counting. Six tables. Nine trees. Four stars in the sky. One full moon.

My knees were shaking.

I pulled out a chair to sit down. The seat banged into the table leg. The whole table shook.

Uh-oh! A dessert plate was set close to the edge of the table. Too close.

CRASH!

The plate hit the ground. And smashed to pieces.

I dropped to my knees to count the pieces. My heart was pounding so hard, my chest ached.

Please, please, don't let there be thirteen pieces! I begged.

I stopped counting at fifteen. I glanced up at Lindy, who was watching anxiously. "It's okay," I told her.

"Be careful, Lucky," my mom called. "Don't cut yourself."

Right, I thought. I'd hate to get a cut that might need thirteen stitches.

My father called the waiter over. "Excuse me— we broke one of your plates," he said. "I'm so sorry." He pulled out his wallet again. "How much do we owe you for that?"

The waiter went inside to check. All I wanted was to get home. Who cared about a stupid plate?

The waiter returned. "I asked my boss," he reported. "He said the plates cost thirteen dollars each."

I froze.

Thirteen dollars.

Thirteen thirteens!

It was over.

I was dead meat.

The evil was on its way.

CHAPTER 13

The sounds of the restaurant faded away.

Silence now. A deeper silence than I had ever known.

The sky darkened to black. A dark cloud formed above the restaurant.

The moon—where was the moon?

My breath caught in my throat. This was it! The darkness. The evil. It was here.

I could feel it...the cloud lowering over me...

The prediction was coming true!

No one else seemed to notice a thing. Not even Lindy. She turned to watch Dad pull money out of his wallet. Her head moved in slow motion. Dad's arm moved even more slowly. I could see his mouth moving. But I couldn't hear his voice.

Silent…It was so silent…

The darkness spread over me like a heavy, black blanket.

I gazed up, shaking in terror. The cloud—it was twisting…sprouting legs. And arms. Lots of them.

I didn't bother to count them. I didn't have to. I knew there were thirteen. Thirteen long, snaky arms.

Claws sprouted out the end of each arm. Sharp, cloud-colored claws, curved like giant fish hooks.

Then a head took shape. An enormous bald head. Bulging eyes. And a huge, open, drooling mouth.

The creature darkened, turned solid. Not a cloud anymore. It hung above the trees, just over the restaurant.

Doesn't anyone else see it? I wondered.

Where can I run? Where can I hide?

The creature stretched out its arms. Its gleaming claws swiped at my head. "Yaaaaiiiee!" I yelled, and ducked.

I'd been frozen in fear. That snapped me out of it.

If that thing wants me, I decided, it has to catch me first!

I leaped up and dived toward the door.

But a few steps later, I felt those horrible claws. Grabbing my shoulders. Digging into my skin.

The creature spun me around. I stared up into its hideous grin. I gagged as its hot, putrid breath poured over my face.

The beast opened its jaws wide. Saliva dripped from the thirteen fangs that lined its mouth.

"Noooo!" I screamed. I struggled wildly.

Then the huge jaws closed around my head. Its fangs dug into my shoulder.

Darkness. Hot and black inside the creature's horrible mouth.

I punched and kicked with all my strength. My foot connected with the monster's chin.

The mouth loosened. I could feel the creature shudder.

I hurt it! I thought. I kicked again. And again. Harder!

The beast shook in wild fits.

Then I realized the truth. The monster wasn't hurt.

It was *laughing*!

The beast's mouth opened as it roared with laughter. I could see around me again.

I stared desperately across the restaurant. Couldn't anybody help me?

Lindy was gazing at me, her face puzzled, confused.

"Help!" I pleaded. "Lindy—please can't you help me?"

She kept staring at me. She couldn't see the monster.

No one could see it—and it was about to swallow me!

As I struggled to free myself, I saw Lindy lean forward over the table. Her arm knocked against a plate.

The plate teetered in slow motion. Then it settled back gently onto the tablecloth.

Yes! Wait!

An idea flashed into my mind.

A desperate idea.

I twisted my left shoulder out of the monster's jaw. My hand shot out.

And knocked Lindy's plate off the table.

It tumbled down, down. It seemed to take forever.

I held my breath.

Would it work?

Would my plan work?

CHAPTER 14

Finally the plate shattered into a million pieces.

Yes! Yes!

"That's *two* broken plates!" I screamed at the monster. "Two plates—that's twenty-six dollars Dad has to pay! Not thirteen. Not thirteen!"

A wave of hot, sour breath poured over me as the monster opened its jaws in a howl of defeat.

I fell to the floor.

The howling creature floated above me...and then faded...faded to vapor.

Sound and light suddenly returned. I heard voices again, the clatter of plates and silverware. Music.

Yes! Yes! I had done it! I had defeated the evil!

"Sorry," the waiter was saying to my dad. "That's two broken plates! I'll have to charge you twenty-six dollars, not thirteen."

My dad sighed. "Try to be more careful, Lucky," he murmured.

I started laughing. I couldn't stop.

Lindy stared at me across the table. "What happened? Tell me!" she demanded.

"It's over," I replied when I could get my breath again. "The evil spirit was here."

"What?" Lindy gasped. "Here? Are you serious?"

"Totally serious. It had me in its jaws! But then I broke the second plate, and that got rid of the last thirteen. I'm safe!"

Dad turned to us. "Time to go," he said, "before Birthday Boy breaks anything else!

I was so happy to get home. I thanked my parents for a great birthday and hurried up to my room.

I was exhausted!

I glanced at my old clock as I climbed into bed. Ten minutes to midnight. I checked my watch.

Yes. For once the old clock was keeping perfect time.

I patted Barker good night and snuggled under the sheets.

I thought about the scene back in the restaurant.

Talk about a narrow escape! I really *was* lucky. Breaking that plate saved me. Saved me from the evil.

I yawned. My eyelids drooped.

Bong. Bong. Bong.

Good old clock. Chiming the hour.

Bong. Bong. Bong.

I opened my eyes and checked my watch. Not quite midnight. The clock was a little early. That figured. It never ran right for long.

I closed my eyes again.

Bong. Bong. Bong. Bong. Bong. Bong.

"Twelve," I murmured. Then I let out a little laugh.

That clock never gets it right!

Bong.

My eyes snapped open.

Huh? Thirteen?

Thirteen chimes?

No!

No…!

Total silence now.

And outside my window the moon suddenly went dark.

Photograph © Dan Nelken

R.L. (Robert Lawrence) Stine is one of the best-selling children's authors in history. His Goosebumps series, along with such series as Fear Street, The Nightmare Room, Rotten School, and Mostly Ghostly have sold nearly 400 million books in this country alone. And they are translated into 32 languages.

The *Goosebumps* TV series was the top-rated kids' series for three years in a row. R.L.'s TV movies, including *The Haunting Hour: Don't Think About It* and *Mostly Ghostly*, are perennial Halloween favorites. And his scary TV series, *R.L. Stine's The Haunting Hour*, is in its second season on The Hub network.

R.L. continues to turn out Goosebumps books, published by Scholastic. In addition, his first horror novel for adults in many years, titled *Red Rain*, will be published by Touchstone books in October 2012.

R.L. says that he enjoys his job of "scaring kids." But the biggest thrill for him is turning kids on to reading.

R.L. lives in New York City with his wife, Jane, an editor and publisher, and King Charles Spaniel, Minnie. His son, Matthew, is a sound designer and music producer.

R.L. STINE'S
THE
HAUNTING
HOUR
THE SERIES.

Don't Let Your Parents Watch it Alone!

Only on The Hub TV Channel!
Visit hubworld.com
for channel listings and showtimes.

Made in United States
North Haven, CT
02 November 2022

26215644R00048